First Experiences
Betty and Jim go to School

Betty

Jim

Published in Great Britain in MMXIII by
Scribblers, a division of Book House
25 Marlborough Place, Brighton BN1 1UB

ISBN: 978-1-908177-39-1

SALARIYA

1 3 5 7 9 8 6 4 2

A CIP catalogue record for this book is available
from the British Library.

Printed and bound in China.
Printed on paper from sustainable sources.

PAPER FROM
SUSTAINABLE
FORESTS

Visit
www.salariya.com
for our online catalogue and
free interactive web books.

First Experiences
Betty and Jim go to School

Margot Channing

At home

Betty and Jim wake up early because they are so excited. Today is their first day at school.

They want to set off now, but Mum says they must start their day with a good breakfast.

Jim

Mum

Betty

Getting ready

After breakfast they brush their teeth. Betty is ready to go but Jim checks his bag one last time. He has a pencil, a ruler, a rubber and his packed lunch — yes, everything's there.

It's time to go!

Jim

Dad

Betty

Getting to school

Jim and Betty's school is only ten minutes' walk from their house. Dad will walk to school with them today.

At the school gate, Dad waves them goodbye and they run inside.

Dad

Jim

Betty

In the cloakroom

Everyone is hanging up their coats and bags in the cloakroom.

The teacher tells Betty and Jim that everyone has a peg with their name written under it. She helps them to find their pegs.

Jim

Betty

Miss Jolly,
the teacher

The classroom

The classroom is bright and sunny with lots of pictures on the walls.

Their teacher is called Miss Jolly. She asks Betty what her name is. Then she asks everyone else in the class.

Lulu

Joe

Jim

Betty

Miss Jolly

Painting time

Miss Jolly wants everyone to paint a picture. They each get a job to do so that the paints, paper, brushes and water jars are handed out quickly. Jim finishes his painting first, so Miss Jolly asks him to help Joe.

Miss Jolly

Lulu

Joe

Jim

Betty

Playtime

It's playtime now, so everyone is in the playground.

Jim is playing football with one of his new friends. They are having fun and getting to know each other.

Jim

Joe

Betty

Lesson time

Miss Jolly has drawn shapes on the whiteboard. She hands out shapes that match up with her drawings.

Miss Jolly tells them the name of each shape: Joe has a triangle, Lulu has a circle, Betty has a star and Jim has a square.

Betty

Miss Jolly

Lulu

Jim

Joe

In the afternoon

Everyone has lunch at school — a packed lunch or a hot meal from the kitchens.

Afterwards, Miss Jolly shows her class how to use the computer. The computer will help them to join up letters to make words. It can help them draw pictures as well.

Betty

Joe

Miss Jolly

Lulu

Jim

P.E. lesson

Now Jim and Betty's class is in the gym for a P.E. lesson. The teacher makes sure that no-one gets hurt.

Miss Jolly blows her whistle when Jim bumps into Lulu. He must sit and watch for five minutes.

Miss Jolly

Joe

Lulu

Betty

Jim

Music time

Everyone plays together.
What a noise!

Then they take turns to play.
The others listen and think of
words to describe each sound.
They think Jim's triangle
sounds quiet and tinkly.

Miss Jolly

Jim

Betty

Lulu

Joe

Story time

The class settles down for story time. Miss Jolly reads the first chapter and then stops. Everyone wants her to read more. Miss Jolly smiles. She promises to read the next chapter at the same time tomorrow.

It's time to go home now!

Betty

Jim

Joe

Miss Jolly

Lulu

Home time

They all wave goodbye to Miss Jolly.

Betty and Jim run to tell Dad all about their first day at school. Betty shows him her painting but says that Joe's painting was even better.

Betty

Jim

Dad

Notes for parents and carers

Your schooldays, they say, are the happiest days of your life. Yet starting school can be an anxious time for children and for their parents or carers. The more you plan ahead, the easier you can make it, both for the child and for yourself.

- Make sure your child has the basic skills to manage without your help for a few hours a day. Children need to be able to go to the toilet by themselves and wash their hands afterwards, to dress and undress for P.E., and to eat without adult help. Of course, teachers will help with these things if necessary, but the more independent the child can be, the better.
- If possible, teach children to recognise their own name when it's written down. This allows them to find their own peg or tray in the classroom or cloakroom.
- Get the child used to the idea of school by telling them about your own schooldays, especially the things you enjoyed and the friends you made. Remind them about any friends of theirs who will be going to the same school, or any siblings or cousins who are already there.
- Children who have already been to nursery school will have a head start. Tell them about the exciting new things they will be doing in 'big' school.
- Walk the child past the school and point out any attractive features such as large toys or play equipment.
- Go to any open days that the school holds. Ask whether your child can spend a day or half-day in school to see what it's like.
- Make sure before the start of term that you have everything your child needs for school. School uniform can be expensive, but the school may be able to advise you where to buy it more cheaply. Some retailers don't stock school uniform after September! Make sure that every item has the child's name on it.
- If the worst comes to the worst and there are tantrums, don't panic and don't blame yourself. Teachers have seen it all before, and they know what to do.

Some helpful websites:
http://www.parentdish.co.uk/back-to-school/starting-primary-school-advice-secondary-prepare-child/
http://www.nhs.uk/Livewell/childhealth1-5/Pages/Firstdayofschool.aspx

Wordlist

breakfast

The first meal of the day. It's very important to have a good breakfast before you go to school, so you don't feel tired and hungry during the morning.

cloakroom

A room where you hang your coat and bag while you are at school. In the winter you also keep your wellies there.

P.E.

A lesson where you play sports and games, either indoors or outside. Some children think this is the best part of the school day — and it helps to keep you strong and healthy, too.

peg

A hook in the cloakroom for you to hang your coat on. Your teacher will write your name next to it so you can tell which peg is yours.

story time

A special time at the end of the day when all the children sit quietly together while the teacher reads a story to them. Your classroom may have a special story corner.

whiteboard

A large white board on a stand, where the teacher can write things for the children to read. Some schools have electronic whiteboards which are like giant computer screens.

Index